THIS WALKER BOOK BELONGS TO:

_____

_____

_____

For Flea, Sara and James

First published 1994 by Walker Books Ltd
87 Vauxhall Walk, London SE11 5HJ

This edition published 1996

10 9 8

© 1994 Kim Lewis Ltd

This book has been typeset in M Baskerville

Printed in China

British Library Cataloguing in Publication Data:
a catalogue record for this book
is available from the British Library

ISBN-13: 978-0-7445-4748-1
ISBN-10: 0-7445-4748-2

www.walkerbooks.co.uk

THE
LAST TRAIN

KIM LEWIS

WALKER BOOKS
AND SUBSIDIARIES
LONDON · BOSTON · SYDNEY · AUCKLAND

On the old railway line stood a hut. Railway men used to have their tea there, when they worked on the line. But now the tracks were gone and the hut was empty.

That very hot summer, sheep used the hut. They rubbed their newly shorn fleeces against the walls and put their heads up the chimney to escape the flies. More and more gaps appeared in the walls. One day the door finally crashed to the ground.

Sara and James stopped on their bicycles to look.

"Let's make a camp," Sara said. She and James left their bicycles and clambered into the hut. They worked all morning, stuffing the cracks with wool and grass and stamping the dirt floor as flat as they could.

They leaned out of the window and dreamed of the last train running through their farm. They thought they could see it, huge and puffing, as it rushed swift and mighty past the old hut. They thought they could hear it, horn wailing and wheels clattering fast on the tracks. They imagined being railway workers and signalled to the driver as he sped by, high up in his cab.

But the wind blew through the gap where the door used
to be and the stuffing fell out of the cracks. The railway hut
looked much as it had before.

"Some camp," declared James. They sadly wheeled
their bicycles home.

Mum and Dad were busy in the sheep pens.
They finished work to sit on the wall.

"The railway hut is going to fall down soon,"
sighed Sara, slumping beside them.

"Will you help us save it?" pleaded James.

It was very hot, but they still set out, with tools
and bits of wood, string and old carpet, bales of
hay, pots and pans, all balanced on James' go-cart.

Sheep gathered to watch, as the cart rumbled
along the railway line to the hut.

Dad and James made a shutter for the window. Mum and Sara made a door. They used the hay bales for seats and laid bits of wood and old carpet on the floor. They worked all afternoon, forgetting about time.

"Look!" James shouted to the waiting sheep. "Look at Railway Cottage now!"

Sara pinned her red handkerchief up by the fireplace.

"Whoever waves this when they stand by Railway Cottage will see a train," she said, "and the driver will stop."

Mum and Dad looked at each other and smiled.

"Tell us all about trains," said James.
He and Sara snuggled up on the bales, as evening drew in, very still and close.

Dad, who remembered steam trains, talked about when he'd watched them as a boy. Mum said she'd seen a photo in the village shop of a steam train stopped at the old village station.

The hot day darkened and a hush seemed to hold the air. Suddenly a gust of wind blew open the shutter.

James scrambled up and
leaned out of the window.
Rain fell on his face.
A crack of lightning split the
hot air, just as low rumbles
swelled from the hills.

Quickly Sara grabbed the
red handkerchief and
flew out of Railway Cottage.

James froze. In a thundering
hiss of steam, a train blew out
of the wind, carrying a wreath
on the front. He watched
unbelieving, as the train grew
bigger and bigger, puffing
slower and slower, steam
billowing out over the
railway line. He saw Sara
wave the red handkerchief.
Rain hissed down on the
hot train, spitting on the metal.

James raced out of Railway Cottage.
He and Sara took turns waving the red
handkerchief. They waved and waved.
The train brakes thundered and squealed.
The driver poked his head out of the
brightly lit window, high up in his cab.
He smiled and waved back.

"Thunderstorm!" shouted Mum and Dad,
stumbling out of Railway Cottage. Rain was falling
in slanting hard drops, faster and faster, pelting on
the tin roof of Railway Cottage. Mum grabbed
Sara and James' hands and pulled them along the
railway line, throwing jumpers over their heads.

In another flash of lightning,
Sara looked back. Railway Cottage
stood by itself, snug against the
rain, a last plume of smoke
curling out of the chimney.

But the railway line was empty
and the train was gone.

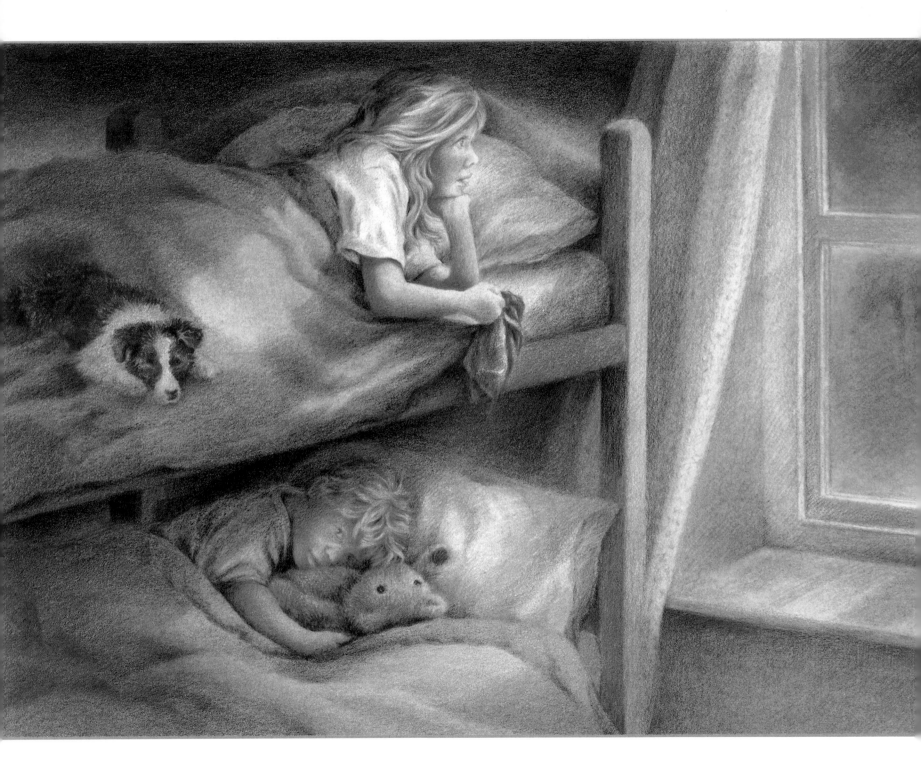

They shook the wet out of their clothes at home, shivering and laughing while it thundered and rained outside.

Mum and Dad tucked Sara and James into bed, but Sara could hardly sleep. She clutched the red handkerchief. James chattered excitedly, "We saw it! We saw the last train at Railway Cottage!"

Mum and Dad kissed them.

"Of course you did…" they said and smiled.

But Sara and James lay awake. They listened for trains in the rain, and whispered to each other in the dark.

WALKER BOOKS BY KIM LEWIS

FLOSS • JUST LIKE FLOSS • EMMA'S LAMB

ONE SUMMER DAY • FRIENDS • MY FRIEND HARRY

THE LAST TRAIN • A QUILT FOR BABY • LITTLE BAA

GOODNIGHT HARRY • HERE WE GO, HARRY

HOORAY FOR HARRY